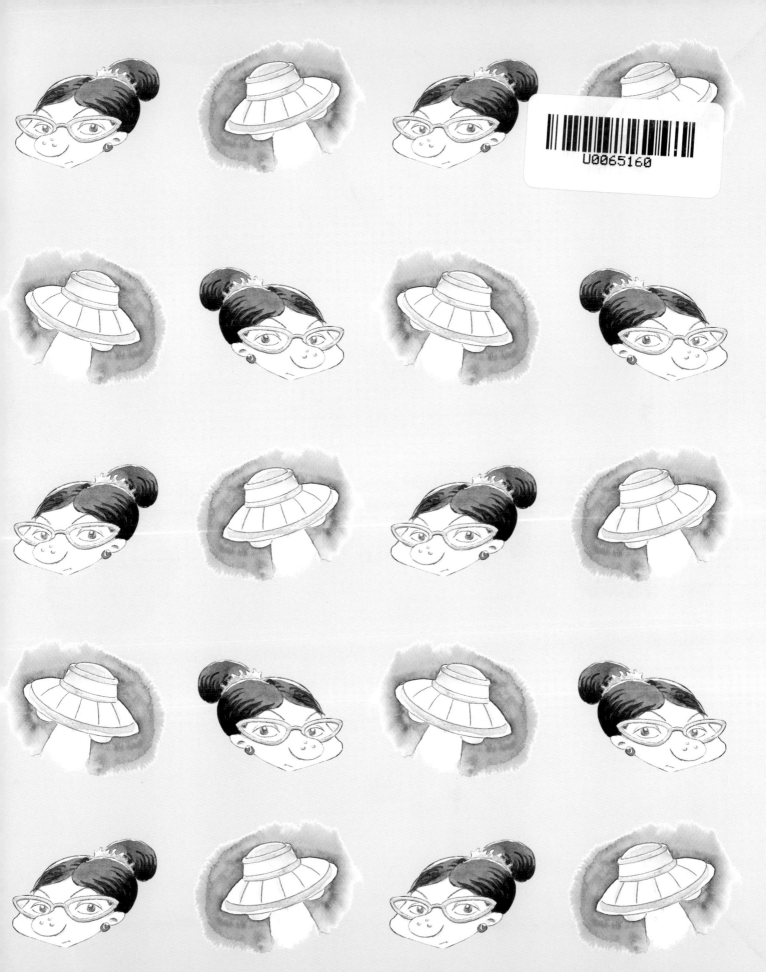

The New Teacher is an Alien
外星老師來上課

Coleen Reddy 著

倪靖、郜欣、王平 繪

蘇秋華 譯

三民書局

For Mr. and Mrs. Kingston

Thank you for your hospitality and support.

致 Kingston 夫婦
感謝你們的照顧與支持

The students at Dogooder Junior High School had a love-hate relationship with Mr. Peemple. He was their English teacher.

1

At times, he could be scary. When he was angry, his face got redder and redder until he looked like he would explode into a million bits.

But just when you thought that he was the meanest teacher in school, he would do something nice. Sometimes he passed students who should have failed by giving them extra points just for writing their names correctly.

That's why when Mr. Peemple took a month long vacation, they were a little sad. In fact, they even missed him. They were going to get a new substitute teacher. They didn't know much about her except that her name was Ms. Dragoen and that she was from Roswell.

When the students heard that she was from a town called Roswell, they were very excited. Everyone knew about Roswell. It was very famous. The people of Roswell said that long ago, an alien spacecraft had crashed in their town. They also said that they saw aliens come out of the UFO. No one knows what happened to the aliens after that; they mysteriously disappeared. Maybe Ms. Dragoen had seen an alien, or maybe she had even seen a UFO. They couldn't wait to meet her.

On Monday morning, everyone was sitting down waiting for the new teacher to arrive. They were all talking about aliens and UFO's.

Suddenly, the door opened and everyone stopped talking. In walked the new teacher. She walked to the front of the classroom and turned around. Oh no! She didn't look friendly. She didn't look like the kind of person that you could talk to about aliens. In fact, she LOOKED LIKE AN ALIEN HERSELF!

Ms. Dragoen was very tall. She was the tallest person the students had ever seen. There was something strange about her head. It was very large; it looked TOO large.

Ms. Dragoen was also very thin. She had long hair that was tied up. But her face was the scariest. It was so white that she looked dead. She had large eyes. Her lips were so thin that you almost couldn't see them. Her nose was also very big and had three moles on it. She wore glasses that made her eyes look even bigger. She didn't smile. She looked mad.

"She's the strangest person I've ever seen," thought Amy Smith.

"Good morning, class. I will be your substitute teacher for a month. My name is Ms. Dragoen. Let's begin," Ms. Dragoen said.

The students all stared. Her voice was the most awful thing. It was a squeaky voice that made you want to cover your ears.

As soon as the class was over, all the students discussed Ms. Dragoen. "Have you ever seen anyone as strange as Ms. Dragoen?" asked David.

"No!" said Jason.

"She doesn't look very friendly. I suppose we can't ask her all about Roswell now," said Amy.

"I don't think Ms. Dragoen will talk to us about aliens," said Kyle.

"Yeah," said David. "She looks like an alien herself."

"That's funny," said Amy. "I was thinking the same thing."

"Do you think she could be an alien?" asked Kyle, laughing.

"Seriously, maybe she's one of those aliens from the UFO," said David.

"No one knows what happened to them; they disappeared," said Amy.

"Or maybe she's the child of an alien. Or maybe she's half alien-half human," said Jason.

Kyle started laughing again.

During lunch, they waited for Ms. Dragoen to leave the classroom. Then they went in and closed the door behind them. They were looking for her purse. It might give them some information about the mysterious Ms. Dragoen.

Amy found Ms. Dragoen's purse on the table and they opened it. They found a letter but it wasn't in English. It was in some STRANGE language.

"It's an alien language," said Jason.

They also found a small device that looked like a
cellphone, but it was too small to be a cellphone. It was
smaller than Amy's palm. Kyle picked it up carefully and
was looking at it when it started moving. Kyle screamed
and dropped the strange thing. They all started screaming
and ran for the door.

But at the same time, Ms. Dragoen came back. She saw the students and she also saw all her things on the desk.

"What are you doing?" she asked in her strange voice. She was mad.

"We wanted to speak to you about…about…about the book that we have to read for English class," said Amy.

"Why were you going through my things ?" she asked.

"Because, because..." said Amy.

"Because we wanted to know if you were an alien. Now we know that you are and we're going to tell the principal," Kyle said boldly.

Then the strangest thing happened. Ms. Dragoen started crying.

Amy, Kyle, David, and Jason looked at each other and Ms. Dragoen. They felt uncomfortable.

"Ms. Dragoen, are you okay?" asked Amy.

"You American children are so mean. How can you think that I am an alien?" asked Ms. Dragoen.

"We found that letter in your purse. It's not written in English so it must be an alien language," said David.

"Yeah, and we also found that thing. It moves! It's alive! We all saw it," said Kyle.

"We also heard that you are from Roswell, the famous alien town," said Jason.

"And you do speak funny," said Amy.

Ms. Dragoen stopped crying and looked up. Then she started laughing.

"What's so funny?" asked Kyle.

"I don't speak funny. I just speak differently. I am not from America. I am from Germany," said Ms. Dragoen.

"Oh!" said David.

"But we heard that you are from Roswell, which is in America," said Jason.

"No, I am from Roswiel, which is a small town in Germany," said Ms. Dragoen.

"What about the strange letter and that moving thing in your purse?" asked Amy.

"The letter is written in German. It is from my mother. And that 'moving thing' is the latest cellphone. I can't take calls when I'm teaching so I had it on 'vibrate mode.' That means it moves instead of ringing," said Ms. Dragoen.

The students felt very stupid and embarrassed.

"We're sorry," said Kyle. "Please forgive us for thinking that you were an alien."

"Okay, you're forgiven. If you don't tell anyone, I won't tell anyone," said Ms. Dragoen.

Amy, Kyle, Jason, and David went home that day, feeling foolish.

Amy was lying in bed that night and thinking about the whole thing when suddenly she jumped out of bed. "Wait a minute," she thought, "Why would someone from Germany come to America to teach English?"

Amy ran to the study and opened an atlas.

"Ah hah!" she thought. "There is no town called Roswiel in Germany." Ms. Dragoen had lied to them.

She immediately phoned David. David phoned Kyle and Kyle phoned Jason.

They decided that tomorrow morning they would tell the principal all about Ms. Dragoen.

But the next day, Ms. Dragoen was gone.

The principal said that she had suddenly become very sick and she would not be their teacher anymore. They would have a new teacher.

"Can you believe it?" asked David. "She must have left because we guessed that she was an alien."

"It was too dangerous for her to stay here because we knew about her, so she lied that she's sick and left the town," said Amy.

"I wonder where she'll go now," said Jason.

"She'll probably try to take over another school now," said Kyle.

"We're lucky that we found out what she was," said Amy.

After that the students were very suspicious of all the teachers. You never knew which one was an alien. They were ALL so weird.

外星老師來上課

督顧德國中的學生和皮波老師維持著一種又愛又恨的關係。皮波老師教的是英文，有的時候，他很恐怖，當他發起脾氣的時候，他的臉會漲得越來越紅，最後簡直像快爆炸了一樣。可是就在學生們認為他是全校最惡劣的老師的時候，他又會做些好事。像是有時候，他會因為學生寫對了他們自己的名字而幫他們加分，讓本來會被當的學生逃過一劫。這也就是為什麼當皮波老師休一個月的長假時，學生都覺得有點難過。說實在的，他們多少有點想念他。雖然學校會派代課老師來幫皮波老師上課，但他們對新老師一無所知，只知道她從羅斯威爾來，姓德拉貢。
（p.1～p.4）

聽到新老師是從羅斯威爾鎮來的時候，學生們都很興奮。大家都聽過羅斯威爾的傳聞，這個小鎮相當有名，因為當地人說很久很久以前，有一艘由外星人所駕駛的太空船墜毀在鎮上。他們還言之鑿鑿地說，有人看到外星人從幽浮裡走出來，之後便神祕地失去了蹤影，沒人曉得外星人後來到底怎麼了。也許德拉貢老師曾經目睹外星人或者是幽浮。同學們都等不及要和她見面了。

(p.5)

星期一早上，全班同學坐在位子上等候新老師大駕光臨。他們興奮地談論幽浮和外星人的事。突然間，門打開了，全部的人立刻安靜下來。新老師走進來，走到講台前，轉過身。噢，不好了，她看起來不怎麼和善，完全不像那種會讓你想跟她討論外星人事件的人。事實上，她看起來就像個外星人。

德拉貢老師非常高大，同學們從沒見過比她還高的人。她的頭看起來怪怪的，體積非常大，大得不像話，而身體卻很瘦，長髮高高地紮在後面。最可怕的是她的臉，白得像僵屍一樣。她有一對大眼睛，嘴唇非常的薄，薄得幾乎快看不見了。她的鼻子也很大，上面還長了三顆痣。她戴的眼鏡有放大效果，使得她的一對銅鈴眼看起來更大。她的臉上沒有笑容，看起來像在生氣。

愛玫・史密斯心想：「她是我見過最古怪的人了。」

德拉貢老師開始自我介紹：「早安，各位同學，這個月將由我來擔任你們的代課老師。我姓德拉貢。好了，開始上課。」

學生們嚇得睜大了眼睛，原來德拉貢老師的聲音才是最可怕的，非常短促、尖銳，使人不由自主想把耳朵摀起來。

（p.6～p.11）

才一下課，學生們就迫不及待地討論起新老師。大維說：「你們有沒有看過比德拉貢老師更怪的傢伙啊？」

杰生說：「絕對沒有！」

愛玫說：「她看起來不怎麼好相處，我想我們不能問她羅斯威爾的事囉。」

凱爾說：「我不認為她會跟我們講外星人的事。」

大維接口：「對啊！她自己就像個外星人。」

愛玫說：「有意思，我也在想同樣的事耶。」

凱爾笑著問大家：「你們覺得她是外星人？」

大維說：「說真的，她八成就是那些搭乘幽浮來的外星人其中之一。」

愛玫說：「沒人曉得那些外星人後來怎麼了，他們就這樣消失了。」

杰生附和：「要不然，她可能就是外星人的後代，或是地球人和外星人的混血。」

凱爾又笑了出來，說：「太扯了啦，你們不會真的相信吧？沒有人能證明是不是真的有幽浮或者外星人。」

愛玫說：「當然有啊，如果沒有的話，為什麼還會有這麼多人相信呢？」

大維則提議：「我想我們該多打聽一些德拉貢老師的事，如果她真是外星人的話，她可能是想佔領學校，然後把我們通通變成外星人。」

吃午飯的時候，他們等德拉貢老師一離開教室，便偷溜進去，把門帶上，開始翻找老師的皮包，看看裡面有沒有什麼線索能夠揭開老師神祕的面紗。愛玫在桌上找到德拉貢老師的皮包，便打開來看。裡面有一封信，寫的不是英文，而是一種陌生的文字。

杰生說：「這一定是外星語言。」

接著，他們又發現一具很小的設備，看起來有點像行動電話，可是體積實在太小了，連愛玫的手都比它大。凱爾小心翼翼地把它拎起來仔細瞧，就在這個時候，那東西動了！凱爾尖叫一聲，連忙把那怪東西甩開。他們四個齊聲大叫，沒命地往門外衝。

巧合的是，德拉貢老師回來了。她先看到一群驚魂未定的學生，然後又看到她桌上的東西被翻得亂七八糟的。

她氣極敗壞地用她古怪的聲音問：「你們在做什麼？」

愛玫說：「我們只是想問妳有關……有關……我們英文課要唸的那本書的事。」

老師又問：「所以你們就隨便亂翻我的東西？」

愛玫結巴了：「因為……因為……」

凱爾鼓起勇氣說：「因為我們想知道妳是不是外星人，現在我們曉得妳是了，我們要去告訴校長。」

(p.18～p.23)

接著，奇怪的事情發生了。德拉貢老師開始嚎啕大哭。

愛玫、凱爾、大維和杰生面面相覷，然後又望著老師，他們覺得很不自在。

愛玫問：「德拉貢老師，您還好嗎？」

老師說：「你們這些美國小孩真壞。你們怎麼會以為我是外星人呢？」

大維說：「我們在妳的皮包裡找到一封信，不是用英文寫的，所以一定是外星文字。」

凱爾說：「對，我們還找到那個怪東西，它會動！它是活的！我們親眼看到的。」

杰生說：「我們還聽說你是從羅斯威爾來的，那個小鎮就是因為外星人才會那麼有名。」

愛玫說：「而且妳說話的樣子真的很奇怪。」

德拉貢老師停止哭泣，抬頭看看他們，接著居然破涕為笑。

凱爾問：「什麼事那麼好笑？」

老師回答：「我講話不是奇怪，只是有腔調而已，我不是美國人，我是從德國來的。」

大維說：「喔！」

杰生說：「可是我們聽說妳是從羅斯威爾來的，羅斯威爾不是在美國嗎？」

德拉貢老師說：「不對，我是從盧斯維爾來的，這在德國是個很小的小鎮。」

(p.25～p.26)

愛玫又問：「那麼，妳皮夾裡那封奇怪的信，還有那個會動的東西又怎麼解釋？」

老師說：「那封信是用德文寫的，是我媽媽寄給我的家書。至於那個『會動的東西』是最新款的手機。上課時我不能接電話，所以調整成震動模式，電話來時它不會響，只會震動。」

學生們覺得自己做了蠢事，糗斃了。

凱爾先向老師道歉：「對不起，請原諒我們，居然把您當作外星人。」

老師原諒了他們：「沒關係，我原諒你們。只要你們不把今天發生的事說出去，我也不會到處去說的。」

愛玫、凱爾、杰生和大維那天回家後，都很後悔做了傻事。但到了夜裡，愛玫躺在床上回想整件事情的始末，突然間，她跳下床，心想：「等一下，為什麼德國人會跑到美國來教英文？」

於是她衝到書房裡翻地圖。

她又想：「啊哈！德國根本沒有什麼叫盧斯維爾的小鎮。」德拉貢老師說謊。

愛玫立刻打電話給大維，告訴他這個驚人的發現。大維再打電話給凱爾，然後凱爾又打電話給杰生。他們決定第二天一早就要把德拉貢老師的祕密告訴校長。

（p.27～p.31）

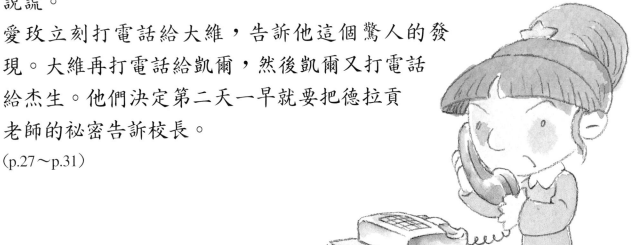

但第二天，德拉貢老師就離職了。

校長說，她突然生了重病，不能再來學校，所以他又幫大家找了個新老師。

大維說：「你們相信這一套嗎？她一定是因為被我們發現她是外星人，所以趕快逃走了。」

愛玫說：「我們已經知道她的身分，如果她還繼續留在這裡就太危險了，所以她才謊稱她生病，連夜逃跑。」

杰生說：「不曉得她現在在哪裡？」

凱爾說：「該不會在嘗試佔領另一所學校吧！」

愛玫說：「還好我們及早發現她的真正身分。」

從這件事以後，學生們開始懷疑每一個老師。你永遠不會曉得哪個老師是真正的外星人，每個都有可能，因為他們個個都是怪胎。

（p.33～p.35）

44

國家圖書館出版品預行編目資料

The New Teacher is an Alien: 外星老師來上課 /
Coleen Reddy著; 倪靖, 郜欣, 王平繪; 蘇秋華譯.－
－初版一刷.－－臺北市；三民，2002
　　面；公分－－(愛閱雙語叢書. 青春記事簿系列)
中英對照
ISBN 957–14–3661–5　（平裝）

805

© The New Teacher is an Alien
——外星老師來上課

著作人　Coleen Reddy
繪　圖　倪靖　郜欣　王平
譯　者　蘇秋華
發行人　劉振強
著作財　三民書局股份有限公司
產權人　臺北市復興北路三八六號
發行所　三民書局股份有限公司
　　　　地址／臺北市復興北路三八六號
　　　　電話／二五○○六六○○
　　　　郵撥／○○○九九九八——五號
印刷所　三民書局股份有限公司
門市部　復北店／臺北市復興北路三八六號
　　　　重南店／臺北市重慶南路一段六十一號
初版一刷　西元二○○二年十一月
編　號　S 85622
定　價　新臺幣參佰伍拾元整
行政院新聞局登記證局版臺業字第○二○○號

有著作權・不准侵害